ROSIE'S STORY

Written by Martine Gogoll   Illustrated by Noela Young

MONDO

First published in the United States of America in 1994 by

MONDO Publishing

By arrangement with MULTIMEDIA INTERNATIONAL (UK) LTD

For information contact:
MONDO Publishing
One Plaza Road
Greenvale, New York 11548

Visit our web site at http://www.mondopub.com

Printed in the United States of America
First Mondo printing, October 1994

99 00 01 020 03   9 8 7 6 5 4 3

Originally published in Australia in 1988 by Horwitz Publications Pty Ltd
Original development by Robert Andersen & Associates and Snowball Educational

Library of Congress Cataloging-in-Publication Data

Gogoll, Martine.
    Rosie's story / written by Martine Gogoll ; illustrated by Noela Young.
      p.   cm.
    Summary: Unhappy because other students in her class make fun of her red hair and freckles, Rosie writes a story about how she feels and discovers that she is not alone.
    ISBN 1-879531-62-3 : $4.95
    [1. Self-acceptance—Fiction. 2. Schools—Fiction.] I. Young, Noela, ill. II. Title.
PZ7.G55845Ro   1994
[Fic]—dc20   94-28975
                                                                CIP
                                                                AC

Rosie Wilson had red hair and freckles. But Rosie wanted
to be different.

"I wish I looked like everyone else," she sighed. "I wish
I didn't have red hair and freckles."

Rosie's grandparents thought she was beautiful. They had photos of her everywhere—on top of the television set, on the piano, and in the hallway.

But this didn't make Rosie feel any better. She simply hated her red hair and freckles.

5

One summer Rosie's family moved. When she started at her new school, there were seventeen other children in her class. Five had blond hair, nine had brown hair, and three had black hair.

Rosie was the eighteenth child, and the only one with red hair and freckles.

The others called her Carrots, Strawberry Shortcake, Firecracker, and even Dragon's Breath.

Rosie was miserable. She didn't let herself cry, but she got a terrible headache from holding back the tears.

"I hate my red hair and I hate my freckles, every single one of them," she said to herself.

Rosie told her parents that the other children at school teased her.

"Oh Rosie, we think you're beautiful," said her mother. "And even if you weren't, what you are like inside is more important than what you look like."

Her father gave her one of his biggest bear hugs and said, "Don't you worry about the others. Just ignore them. They'll soon get tired of teasing you."

Rosie hoped that what her parents said was true, but
every school day was the same.
"Hi, Sparky."
"Keep away from the redhead match. You'll get burned!"

"Run. . . fire. . . run!"

Every evening Rosie spent an extra long time in the bath. She tried to scrub the freckles off her arms and legs.

Every night she wished on a star that the color of her hair would change.

But every morning she looked in the mirror and saw the same freckles,
the same red hair,
the same sad little face.

One day Ms. Clarke, Rosie's teacher, announced a picture storybook competition she wanted them all to enter. Each child was to write a story, make it into a book, and bring it to school the following week.

That night, Rosie sat at the kitchen table and sobbed.
"Whatever is the matter, Rosie?" her mother asked.
"I have to write a book for school, and I can't. My head
is full of sadness. No ideas will come. There's no more
space. I'm just an ugly girl with hundreds of freckles."

15

"Why don't you write about how you feel? It might make you feel better, and it might help people understand," Rosie's mother suggested.

"The others would think I'm silly," said Rosie. "They'd laugh at me."

"Why not give it a try anyway," said her mother.

Rosie didn't like the idea, but she couldn't think of anything else.

Rosie didn't want to draw attention to herself, so she decided to write about a boy with red hair and freckles. She called him Rusty.

The following week everyone brought their books to
school.

Thomas read a story called *The Frog Who Wore
Spectacles*. Everyone giggled at the funny parts.

Then Eartha read a mystery. Everyone clapped because
the ending was such a surprise.

Alice read spooky ghost stories which made everyone squirm and gave them goose bumps.

Then it was Rosie's turn.

She read her story in a low voice.

Nobody giggled. Nobody clapped. Everyone looked down at the ground in silence.

Rosie waited. The teacher waited.

Finally Ms. Clarke said, "Well done Rosie. Your story meant a lot to me. When I was a girl I was so skinny, people joked that I would blow away! I know exactly how Rosie—I mean Rusty—must have felt."

Polly raised her hand. "I do too," she said, blushing. "I used to be plump, and everyone called me Dumpling. People even laughed when I ate ice cream."

"People tease me because I like to tap dance," said Carlos. "But tap's not soppy. It's really hard to get the steps right. But when I do, I feel great. If people are mean about it, I just picture them lining up to see me when my name is in lights!"

And Sally added, "When I first got my glasses, I was called Four-eyes. I raced home from the bus stop and threw my glasses in the trash."

"I felt like Rusty when people laughed at me because I didn't understand multiplication," said Mayah.

"Same here," said Andrew.

"You see, everyone feels bad when people make fun of them," said Ms. Clarke. "Understanding that you should think of other people's feelings is one of the most important lessons you can ever learn."

The children finished reading their stories. Then everyone voted for the one they liked best.

Ms. Clarke counted the votes for each story and announced, "The favorite story was written by Rosie Wilson!"

Someone shouted "Good for you, Rosie!" The others clapped and cheered.

Rosie's face went as red as her hair, and for a moment her freckles disappeared!